A CLASSIC BEGINNER'S MISTAKE

PHILIP BREWER

AUTHOR'S NOTE

Swords are cool.

That was the beginning of this story. Swords are cool, and fighting with swords is cool, but I didn't want people killing one another, so I wanted a world where people could fight with swords and hardly ever kill one another.

Another thing that's cool is pocket universes. The pocket universe in this story actually predates the story. But all I had was a cool pocket universe, and no story. But when this story called for a pocket universe, I thought, "Hey! I've *got* a pocket universe I can use!"

One thing that's not cool, but can be interesting, is vast disparities in wealth. And when I wondered *why* people would fight with swords, even if they (probably) weren't risking their lives, that seemed like it might be a motivation.

A CLASSIC BEGINNER'S MISTAKE

E IGHT MINUTES BEFORE MY BOUT, and I was struggling with my goggles — the one really important piece of protective gear. A rapier through the heart is a legitimate medical emergency, but one that the on-site medical staff handle with routine ease. Only a rapier into the brain is at all likely to produce a career-threatening injury and, except for the very rare fluke of a thrust through the soft pallet or the ear, the skull provides enough protection that just about the only way into the brain is through the eye socket.

Hence, goggles.

Walking past the club's pro shop, I'd decided to spring for new, top-of-the-line goggles. Having spent most of my pre-bout time trying to get the package open, now I was trying — with limited success — to get the strap adjusted.

The locker room was oversized, with ample room for an ice bath, a whirlpool bath, both a wet and a dry sauna, and a massage table, as well as a medical examining table under a seal to keep it sterile until an injured fencer needed it. There was ample room for any number of trainers, coaches, masseurs, personal physicians, and other assorted hangers on, but I was alone. It was just me and my rapier.

And the goggles.

Having never had a coach — unless you counted my high school Phys Ed teacher — I didn't really feel the lack. Except that I really wished someone would pop in and get my goggles adjusted to fit.

I had finally gotten them snugged up, only to find that they were pinching my nose and cutting into the back of my head. I loosened them just a tiny bit, and now they were loose enough to leave a gap at the temple plenty big enough for a rapier to slide in.

I was trying to find a spot halfway between when a guy wearing a fightmaster's vest poked his head through the door opposite where I'd entered.

"Trevo? You're up."

I pulled the goggles on. Miraculously, they seemed to fit.

Stripped to the waist, wearing just tights and thin-soled shoes, I walked to the door.

The guy at the door — up close I could see the assistant fightmaster insignia on his shoulder — gave me a look with equal parts sympathy and disdain. He blocked the doorway with his body, pointing to my rapier next to my street clothes.

I thanked him and went back to get it. Once I had it in my hand, he ushered me through the door.

I didn't find myself in the hall I'd expected. The door led directly out onto the fighting floor.

Blinking at the arena lighting, I tried to remember the list of things to check. The only one that came to mind was the floor itself, which was a standard composite, same as the floor of the salle where I'd just started practicing. Unsurprising, since both belonged to the same fencing club.

I had already warmed up and stretched, although not as much as I should have due to the misadventure with the goggles. Now I advanced, lunged, and pulled back, then advanced, lunged, and advanced again — all the while trying not to feel like I was aping the moves of an experienced fencer.

Then the door opposite me opened and my opponent emerged.

He stood taller than me, with longer arms and longer legs. He was also bigger than me, but beefy as much as muscular. Even so, the arena lights made the muscles of his chest gleam and highlighted the swell of his biceps alarmingly.

He advanced to his mark, and I advanced to mine. On the commands from the assistant fightmaster, we saluted one another, went *en garde*, and started fencing.

Fortunately, he wasn't very good. Strong, but not quick.

I fought conservatively for most of a minute, parrying his thrusts, being cautious with my repostes, out of fear he might be better than he seemed.

Around the end of that first minute, I saw his expression change. Saw that he'd come to the conclusion that he was overmatched. Saw him gather himself for a rush.

I seized the opportunity to advance, lunge, and thrust my blade into his abdomen just below his sternum.

It was a good thrust, sinking a good five or six centimeters into his guts.

Concerned that he might be strong enough to still make a fight out of it, I pulled my blade out and retreated a step, but it was over. He just stared at the blood running down his belly, lowered the tip of his blade, and sank to his knees. He tried to turn and look toward the door where the medic should be, then whimpered as if twisting his body hurt.

He leaned forward gingerly, let the grip of his rapier slip free, then put both hands on the floor in front of him.

All at once, the assistant fightmaster called the end of the bout, the medic rushed out, and another figure in fightmaster colors came onto the floor. With practiced attention to the possibility that I might still be wrapped up in the match and ready to stick my rapier into someone else, he gestured back to the same door I'd entered through.

"Trevo? Congratulations. Your match. One point to you. Let's get you checked out and tally your win."

I heard a smattering of applause as I walked back toward the locker room. I looked up and was surprised to see a small audience.

Certainly none of them were there to see me. Maybe a few were friends of my opponent. Maybe one or two were other people in the same match, looking to see how their future opponents fought. The rest, I supposed, were people killing time before or after a bout they'd come to see.

Inside the locker room, the fightmaster gave me a once-over, looking to see if I had any puncture wounds that I hadn't noticed in the excitement of my victory.

Finding me uninjured, he took my fingerprint, then left me to change into street clothes.

By the time I was ready to leave, my match score had been updated to show my single victory.

My club account had also been incremented by two florins. It was a tidy sum, a month's rent, or about a third of the membership fee for the fencing club, which had been provisionally waived against my match winnings. Since I couldn't afford to join the club otherwise, it was a pretty good deal.

•　　　•　　　•

I spotted the great man the moment I walked into the common room. At the center of the throng, all faces turned toward him like flowers following the sun.

I joined the throng. Trying not to be a jerk about it, but determined, I worked my way toward the center.

The man was holding forth about trail running at ultra-marathon distance. "Not my sport," he said, gesturing at his broad chest and shoulders, inviting us to imagine lugging all those kilos of muscle up and down mountain paths, "but a great workout. A whole new kind of leg strength, compared to what you get from squats."

The men in the group all nodded. A few of the women as well, but most of them just gazed at the way his khakis hugged his hips and thighs.

"Are you going to race the Red Canyon 100?" a girl asked, naming the upcoming local ultra-marathon.

"I'm going to run it," Vergil replied turning the full wattage of his attention to the girl, a pretty blonde who promptly started blushing. "And I'm going to register," he added, broadening his attention back to the full crowd. "I find the *frission* of competition brings out the best in me. But I hesitate to call it racing, because of course I won't win. The winner will be someone young and skinny, like this guy."

That last was directed at me, as I reached the innermost circle.

The great man put out a hand toward me. "I'm Virgil Renard."

"Trevo Fisher," I said, taking his hand, refraining from commenting on the preposterousness of him introducing himself.

"I don't believe I've seen you here before."

The intensity of his gaze made it seem entirely likely that he genuinely knew every person in the room, perhaps every person he had ever met.

"I work for Odessa Rae Clover," I said. "She said you'd found a bug —"

"Odessa Rae! She sent you to fix my training golem? That's wonderful!"

Without him seeming to gesture at all, somehow everyone knew to shift around just a bit, making room for me on the sofa just to the right of Virgil's chair.

As I took a seat, Virgil launched into a story about his last 100-kilometer race, featuring some guy who caught up with him a bit more than halfway through, who would not shut up about there being "only one marathon left" before the end.

Virgil made a good story of it. "I tried slowing down, but the guy seemed to have no interest in pressing on for the finish. I tried speeding up, but the guy matched my pace with ease."

About this time someone brought Virgil a drink, and shoved a glass of the same — some rum drink — into my hand as well.

Virgil was wrapping up his story. "Finally, I offered to buy him a beer at the finish line, if he'd just run off and leave me alone. He suggested that two beers would be a fair price and, when I agreed he took off just like he hadn't already run sixty kilometers. He went on to finish 6th, and was waiting at the finish line to claim his two beers."

Virgil kept to the theme of long-distance running for a while, long enough for me to finish that drink and another. I was nursing a third when he turned to me and said, "How about you? You look like a runner."

"I do run," I said.

"And race?"

I smiled. "I race as well," I admitted. "But only at non-standard distances," I said. "There are a lot of little local races where the distance is just however far it is — from one town to the next or around the lake."

"Ah," Virgil said. "So you don't have a best 10k time."

"Exactly!" I said, pleased he understood. "Just a best six-mile time. And a best 7.2 mile time."

Something about his attention thwarted my efforts to nurse that third drink, and pretty soon I found myself with a fourth drink in my hand. I was resolutely limiting myself to very occasional sips, but was already pretty drunk.

Perhaps that was why, the next time he finished a story, I said, "Odessa Rae suggested that, if you were in a mood to tell stories, I ask about the quarter-final bout between you and Max Mandrill. Where you're *corps-a-corps* and he whispers something in your ear."

Virgil gave me a look that suggested it was the wrong sort of question to have asked. The rest of the audience recognized it as well, and a lot of faces turned toward me. For a moment, I felt like maybe I was getting a tiny taste of what it must be like for Virgil all the time. He clearly relished it. I found it a little uncomfortable.

More uncomfortable was getting Virgil's full attention. "Do you fence?" he asked.

"In school," I said.

"But not in the open matches?"

"No."

"I'll tell you what," he said. "Fight in one open match — just five bouts, enough to get a TSO rating. Then come back, and I'll tell you."

Then he swept an arm around to take in the lodge where everyone was gathered. "Stick around! Have some drinks! Enjoy the party! Breakfast will be at six o'clock, and I'll be heading home right after. We can travel together."

By home, of course, Virgil meant his pocket universe.

Just like everyone had understood when I arrived that a place was to be made for me at the center, I understood now that my time at the center was over. Taking care not to spill my almost-full fourth drink, I made my way to the periphery of the throng around Virgil.

I lingered for a while. Virgil was talking about sailing now, about a year he spent living aboard a small sail boat, moving up and down the Sea of Cortez, putting in at this or that Mexican city and working at whatever job he could — which seemed to alternate between construction and bodyguard. He spoke eloquently of a Mexican beauty he met in Cabo San Lucas who nearly convinced him to sell his boat and move ashore with her, until it turned out she was in the employ of a banking syndicate looking to make a connection to the Renard family money.

It was a great story, and I was so focused I almost didn't notice that another beauty — this one looking more Russian than Mexican — had sat down next to me. As Virgil segued into telling a joke that somehow managed to lighten the mood of his story, while simultaneously speaking eloquently of the pain of betrayal, the woman leaned her head against my shoulder in a way that caused her platinum hair to cascade down my chest.

I put my arms around her, and she put her lips to my ear and said, "My name's Ulyana."

"Um," I said, then got my brain got going well enough to at least manage to say, "My name's Trevo."

She moved her head enough to show me her face, which gave me a slightly sardonic grin. "I know. You introduced yourself to Virgil."

"Of course," I said.

She moved her mouth back to my ear and said, "I have a room here at the lodge. How about we go there, until until it's time for you to meet Virgil in the morning?"

I glanced around the room, which was still packed with a lively crowd of Virgil's guests. Outside the sun was still well above the horizon in the western sky.

"I know it's early," she said, "but if you're going to spend the day with Virgil tomorrow, you'll need your sleep."

"Will I get any?" I asked pulling her closer.

"Probably some," she said.

When I stood, she pulled herself close, wrapping her legs around my waist. It made her into a compact bundle that wasn't too hard to lift. She seemed very pleased to be carried as far as the base of the stairs, but there let her legs slide down and stood on her own feet, saying, "I don't want you all worn out before we even get to the room."

•   •   •

Unluckily for me, my second opponent was much better than my first.

He was young. He looked about 14, although he must have been 17 to have entered the tournament.

We went *en garde* and fenced for perhaps ten seconds, at which point he did a fancy encirclement of my blade, corkscrewed forward, and got his tip a centimeter or so into my forearm.

It hurt a lot, and blood started to flow toward my grip, which wasn't going to help anything.

I retreated two steps and he let me. Which I guess made sense. With a hole in my arm, time was most definitely not on my side.

I advanced again, engaged again, got encircled again, took a second thrust in exactly the same spot on my arm.

This time it hurt a lot more.

"My minister says I have to pink you three times on the forearm before I can go for the chest," the boy said.

"Oh," I said.

"He says it's the Christian thing to do."

"Oh," I said again.

"He says I should call on you to yield, after the third."

"Okay," I said.

The boy tried the same encirclement maneuver, and this time I was ready for it, but he just used the force of my perry to reverse the encirclement and come right in to my forearm again. He didn't manage to hit the exact same spot this time, leaving a second puncture wound about one centimeter over.

"Having taken first, second, and third blood," the boy said in a voice pitched to carry to the audience, "I call on you to yield."

"You betcha," I said, lowering my blade and raising my other hand. "I yield. The bout is yours."

I had three more bouts to contest to get my rating, and a chest wound would probably take me out of the tournament.

I didn't get two florins this time, just two quick dabs of wound-sealing gel. When I checked my bank balance, I saw it had been credited one denarius, which would just about cover bus fare, if it weren't being held against the membership fee in the club.

●　　　●　　　●

I slipped out of bed, leaving Ulyana asleep. She'd made clear that she had no interest in saying goodbye at 6:00 AM.

Except for Virgil himself seated alone at a table for two, none of the throng was up at that hour.

A long buffet was laid with hot and cold cereal, yoghurt, potatoes (both roasted and hash-browned), every kind of tropical fruit I knew and several kinds that I didn't recognize, five kinds of bread and rolls, and six kinds of smoked meat. But before I could sample anything, Virgil waved me to the seat across from him and a matronly woman in a white uniform brought me a big plate of eggs, bacon, and pancakes.

"Eat up," he said. "We've got a long day ahead. The bug I reported only shows up when I use both the coaching software and the training golem, and only when I use the golem for a late-afternoon fencing session. That means going through a full day's training. How long have you worked for Odessa Rae?"

I'd been about to ask for details of the bug and took a moment to wrap my head around his question. "Less than a year," I said. "You know that she end-of-lifed the training software, right? Only a handful of people, like you, who bought the lifetime contract are still getting support. The software was very stable and she hardly ever got bug reports, but about a year ago she was right in the middle of a new project and didn't want to drop it to handle a support call. She contracted the work out to me, was pleased with my work, and put me on contract to handle all the support."

"Ulyana is very flexible, isn't she?"

Once again it took me a moment to adjust to the change in subject, but as soon as I did — as soon as I began to think about the creativity, vigor, and enthusiasm that Ulyana had shown that night — I felt my face redden.

"She invited you to her room, right?"

"Yes," I admitted.

Virgil smiled. "And it didn't even occur to you to notice that it was *your* room?"

"My room?"

"This lodge — the Colorado egress point for my pocket universe — has twelve guest bedrooms plus the master suite. Since Odessa Rae had told me you were coming, I'd put aside one of the rooms for your use. Ulyana wanted to spend the night, but had not been invited, so she looked around for a single guy who had been, glommed onto him, and convinced him that she was inviting him to her room, rather than the other way around."

"Huh," I said.

"It's fine, of course," Virgil said. "At least, it's fine with me. And knowing Ulyana — she dances, you know, and teaches yoga — I expect it's fine with you, too. But I thought you ought to know what had happened."

"Thank you, I guess."

We ate in silence then for a few minutes. Virgil finished, waited while I stuffed down my last bites, then stood and walked briskly to the foot of the stairway. At almost the same spot where Ulyana had slid herself down my body to head upstairs, Virgil turned to go down to the basement level.

About half a floor down, a shimmery membrane that looked like the surface of a soap bubble crossed our path. I could see stairs through the membrane, and couldn't tell if they were further stairs, or a reflection of the stairs we'd just come down.

Before I had much time to think about it, Virgil pushed through the membrane, and I followed just a step behind.

•　　•　　•

There were always fencing matches. Every town had a club. Every city had several.

Any fencer could get a fight — that's why they were called open matches. Any fencer with a TSO rating could get a fight against someone of roughly equivalent ability, that being the whole point of having ratings.

I had entered a special, entry level match specifically for unrated fencers. Only unrated fencers were eligible, and the duration — five bouts — was designed so that, win or lose, anyone who made it to the end would emerge with a TSO rating.

Pairings for bouts were arranged with somewhat conflicting goals. First, to have a definitive winner, unbeaten players were paired against one another until at most one person was unbeaten. Secondarily, an effort was made to save the most exciting bouts — the one that would determine the match champion — for the last round.

That was usually pretty easy, when the fighters were rated. It was somewhat trickier with unrated fighters. With little information to go on, it was entirely possible for the two best fighters to get paired up in the first or second round.

Of course, it didn't matter much. It's not like there was big money in live-streaming the championship bout between two unrated fighters. If the match turned out to be a great one, the club and TSO could retro-stream it.

If they did, the fighters got a pittance of the streaming fees, on top of their prize money.

The door opened, and my opponent came out. He was a kid, just a little older than the one I'd fought previously.

To an extent, the pressure was off. I had already lost a bout, which made it very unlikely I could win the match. I had already won a bout, which had confirmed my provisional membership. If I won two more matches, I'd have my membership comped for a year. If I didn't, I could quit and owe nothing, or I could enter another match and keep trying to accumulate three wins.

Very few people earned a living at fencing, but plenty of people earned enough to make the activity pay its way — covering the cost of memberships, training, clothing, and equipment.

Courtesy of rich people wanting to watch poor folks stick one another with swords.

This new kid and I came *en garde* and started fencing.

My opponent seemed to have some skills, but he wasn't moving well — wobbly and slow. I fought conservatively, then gradually picked up the pace. I started working my way around him, which seemed to give him further trouble.

He kept putting his hand on his stomach, rather than keeping it back out of the way. Then I noticed his red eyes and pasty complexion, and decided I had a pretty good idea what had happened.

"Your birthday yesterday?" I asked.

"Yeah?" he said.

"Congratulations," I said, reversing the direction I was circling and picking up the pace as much as I could, fairly hopping around him.

"Thanks?" he said.

"No thanks needed," I said abruptly reversing direction again, but only going one step this time. Then

I planted a foot, lunged, and sank my blade in between two of his lower ribs.

I'd had it in my head that I'd wish him a happy birthday, but decided it would be sort of a dick move. Instead, I just pulled my blade out and backed away.

This match ended the same as the first — injury check, fingerprint, two florins in my club account.

•   •   •

I almost stumbled as I crossed the egress point, because the stairs started up again. Going up about half a floor brought us into a large open-plan main floor done in wood and stone, not too different from the Colorado lodge.

Big windows looked out over land that sloped gently down toward a lagoon, with what looked like open ocean beyond it. Turning around, I saw windows facing the opposite direction that looked out on a small orchard. A mountain stretched up behind it.

I had read up on Virgil's universe.

According to the magazine articles, it was a sphere 14 kilometers in diameter. The top half of the sphere held the habitat: a house surrounded by gardens, some fields planted in crops, a few small ponds, more than 10,000 hectares of forest, and a few small mountains near the center — the biggest stretching up 2,000 meters, meaning that it got almost a third of the way to the roof of the universe.

Around the perimeter, a ring of ocean-blue salty water about fifteen meters wide separated the land from the end of the universe, which was a sky blue color. The fifteen meters was far enough, and the edge of the universe featureless enough, that binocular vision provided no sense that the horizon was closer than it would have been on Earth.

A downward acceleration of 9.8 meters per second squared was a universal constant, providing gravity. There was no star, but a bright disk that moved across the roof of the universe for about twelve out of every twenty-four hours was another universal constant, providing illumination that was quite similar to sunlight at sea level on earth.

The bottom half of the sphere held the equipment to support the habitat, and to maintain the connection to Universe Zero.

"The salle and the fencing golem are on the second floor," Virgil said. "There's a datapoint there where you should be able to turn on logging or whatever you do. Once that's done, come on back down and we can run through the day's workout."

Turning on logging was exactly what I needed to do. It took only a moment, but already by the time I got downstairs Virgil was outside, listening to the coaching system's avatar.

"This morning's workout is dead simple," the avatar said, the projection looking a little ghostly in the full daylight. "Just run to the top of the southern mountain via the southern trail and back down the western side. The elevation change is only 1000 meters, so it shouldn't kill you. Although," the avatar added, making a show of looking at a wristwatch — a huge stainless steel monstrosity, it looked like in the projected image, "the plan was for you to start rather earlier in the morning. Sorry if your lunch is delayed. Oh, and do keep your heart rate under 150. This *moderate* workout is to provide leg training for your ascents and descents. Don't go turning it into speedwork just because you're hungry."

Odessa Rae had told me that the default coaching avatars were based on depictions of drill sergeants drawn from a variety of movies of the latter half of the twentieth century. This one had a working-class English accent and spoke with a modicum of respect.

Seeming satisfied, Virgil started along the path to the mountain, running at an easy pace.

I ran alongside. The path from the garden toward the mountain was broad enough for two to run abreast.

"Do you use Odessa Rae's software for your own training?" Virgil asked.

"Her software is no longer available," I said. "The only people still using it are those few early customers like you who paid for lifetime support."

"Next time your contract comes up for renewal, you should insist on a free copy. And use it. It's a great product. I used to run a lot when I was your age, but then cut back because I wanted more muscle, and couldn't manage the necessary lifting regimen and keep up the running volume as well. It was only with Odessa Rae's training software that I found a way to build my physique *and* run ultra-marathons. It's all about high-quality, low-mileage training."

By the last sentence, Virgil had started breathing a bit harder. The path had begun to wend its way uphill, turning just a bit on a course that would take us all the way around the mountain before we reached the top.

The coaching avatar showed itself for just a moment, shouting as we approached a switchback.

"Perhaps if you'd shut up for a minute, you could get your heart rate back down! It's 156!"

I didn't understand the appeal of software that yelled at me, but Virgil smiled slightly, fell silent, and continued on at a steady pace.

It took a full hour to reach the top, at which point the coaching software called for a short break. We walked for several minutes and drank water from a mountain spring.

Once Virgil was breathing normally again — which didn't take long — the software avatar led him through a stretching routine that might have been some form of yoga that I didn't recognize. I followed along as best I could, which was not very well. Despite his huge musculature, Virgil was much more flexible than I, as well as being more controlled and precise in his movement.

The stretching ended with twenty minutes of seated meditation, after which the coaching avatar said, "You're warmed up, you're stretched out, you're as focused as you ever get. Perhaps the lure of lunch will convince you to go for it on the downward leg, unlike anything I've ever been able to do. Let's see what you can do!"

Virgil started walking briskly toward a path different from the one we'd come up.

I hurried to keep up, then hesitated when I saw that although there was a slight zigzag to it, the path went almost straight down the mountain.

"Feel free to go back down the way we came," Virgil said. "And if you choose to come down this way ... Don't try to keep up."

Then he headed down at a terrifying pace, dancing down the side of the mountain in what was more a controlled fall than a run, his feet just touching down for an instant to keep him on the path.

After that, I didn't think I had any choice but to follow.

In about a minute, my quads started burning. Slowing my pace just made it worse. Speeding up took a bit of the pressure off the quads, but seemed more and more foolish as my legs got more and more tired.

Finally I skidded to a stop so I could rest for a minute. Despite the stretching I'd just done, I felt very much like I needed some more. As I paused to stretch, I looked up, and saw that I'd come down perhaps 100 meters.

The next nine hundred were as hard and painful as anything I'd done before.

Once I got to the bottom, I hobbled the kilometer or so to the house. Virgil was sitting in the garden painting a watercolor of a wilted iris.

As I arrived, a robot servitor brought out a tray with a large salad, a sandwich, a small dish of cottage cheese, and a beer.

"There are a couple of pools around to the side of the house," Virgil said. "The pool to the north is fed by snowmelt off the mountain. It's very cold water, and will do your knees and ankles a world of good. The pool to the south is fed by a hot spring, and is just the way to warm up and loosen up after the icy bath. If you want my advice, I suggest you take a short soak in each. Then have lunch, enjoy your beer, and take a nap in the hammock. When you wake up, I'll show you the bug."

•   •   •

The club I had joined — provisionally joined — had three tiers of fighting floors, distinct from the training spaces and workout rooms.

The top tier, used for important matches, had extensive seating. Just above eye-level around the floor were a few rows of comfortable chairs. Above and behind those were ordinary chairs squeezed somewhat closer together. Yet further away was bleacher seating.

The bottom tier fighting floor, where I'd fought my previous bouts, was tucked away in a back corner of the facility. They had just a few benches for anyone who wanted to watch.

This bout, for the first time, I was fighting in the middle tier, where the fighting floors were adjacent to the bar. Each had bleachers on two sides, but they weren't much used, because there were rarely that many people who wanted to watch the sort of bout that happened in these spaces. But the other two sides fronted onto the lounge area where members could sit, drink a cocktail, and watch people fight.

A few of the audience looked to be fencers who had thought it reasonable to follow a workout with a juice drink or a beer. Others perhaps were celebrating a victory or lamenting a loss — with an appropriate beverage — while watching some of the other members fight.

But many of the people sitting in the lounge did not look like fencers. I had known that you didn't have to fence to be a member. Plenty of rich people joined fencing clubs, but used them like fitness centers or country clubs. Others had some historical connection with fencing — some were former tournament fencers. There were also social fencers — they fenced with foils rather than rapiers, using fencing as a fitness or social activity. Many a business deal was struck over crossed foils. But judging from what I could see as I waited for my opponent, a solid half of the men in the bar, and at least as high a proportion of the women, had probably not fenced since college, if then.

Admittedly, I was basing this on meager evidence: stereotypes, fashion choices, body shape, the look in their eyes as they looked down at me. But I was inclined to trust my judgement on this. There were people looking on — well-fed, well-dressed people — who would never risk their own skin, but were happy enough to sip cocktails, hoping to see me or my opponent run through with a sword.

My opponent emerged from the locker room on the other side, and I let my attention slide from the audience to her.

I hadn't faced a woman before, not since college, and only a few then.

She wore a sports bra in addition to tights similar to what male fencers wore. The fight masters would have verified that the material was not armored, making it rather the opposite of protection — basically, the material was just something to get caught and dragged into the wound, making extra work for the medics if a thrust went through it.

She was fit. Muscled arms and shoulders. Flat stomach.

As soon as the fightmaster started the bout, I could tell she had skills, too. And she wasn't drunk or hungover, like my previous opponent.

I was forced into defensive play — parrying, retreating, circling, keeping her back as best I could with feints and the occasional thrust.

She probably could have taken me. She was fit enough that I wouldn't have been able to wear her out, and skilled enough that I probably wouldn't have scored on her. But I got lucky.

She launched an attack very similar to a move she'd executed twice before. I'd parried it the same way the first two times, but this time I tried a different parry, using it to set up a quick riposte.

The riposte wouldn't have worked; she was too quick. Worse, my parry wasn't good enough and, instead of guiding her rapier past me, she guided her rapier tip right to my face.

The lucky part was that the tip of her rapier landed dead center on the left lens of my goggles — the fancy new goggles I'd bought for my first bout — then caught on their rim.

Her rapier stuck, if only for a moment, the woman tried to pull back. But my riposte had already been launched. Twisting away, she almost escaped it, but I muscled the blade in, trying for a hit anyway, and managed one. It was pretty small, but it caught her on the neck, and apparently nicked the carotid.

Blood didn't fountain, but it did spurt. A narrow stream, like from a pin-prick hole in a hose, shot from her neck in time with her heartbeat.

She very reasonably dropped her sword and clamped her hands on her throat.

The fightmaster stopped the fight, giving me the victory.

The audience — especially the well-dressed contingent I had observed earlier — seemed very pleased. They cheered. They raised glasses in my direction. Behind them, the fencers among the crowd — wearing street clothes, but with gym bags at their feet — made smaller gestures of congratulations. They knew my win had been luck, and they could see I knew it too.

But, they seemed to be saying, luck was something to be congratulated too.

Once again, I was checked for wounds, fingerprinted, and credited with two florins.

My membership was paid up for the year, plus a little. I could probably afford to buy a drink at the club bar. As long as it wasn't a fancy one.

•　　•　　•

I woke up in the hammock feeling surprisingly refreshed. As best I could tell from the glowing disk that crossed the roof of Virgil's pocket universe, it was already mid-afternoon, maybe a little later.

I found Virgil upstairs in the salle — a large, high-ceilinged room comprehensively equipped for combat-related fitness activities. He was practicing shoulder rolls in a quarter of the room outfitted with mats suitable for tumbling or wrestling. A second quarter had a speed bag, a heavy bag, and a wooden martial arts post. The other half of the room was a broad clear space that included a marked fencing strip, but also plenty of room for fighting not restricted to a strip.

A fencing golem stood at the far end, the rapier in its hand held up in a salute, an orange safety button at the tip of the blade.

"You've got your logging all set up?" Virgil asked, coming smoothly out of a roll onto his feet. "As you see, it takes all day to reproduce this bug, so I want to be sure you get everything you need to fix it."

"All set," I assured him, having done that before our run.

"All right, then. Watch."

He moved to a rack of weapons, selected a rapier, then said, "Sergeant, fencing practice."

The coaching avatar appeared, less ghostly indoors than it was outside. "Shall we give level 88 a try, then?"

"No. Level 87."

The avatar gave him a look of pitying disgust, presumably intended to shame a student into stepping up to a challenge, but just said, "Fencing practice. Golem at level 87."

Stepping smoothly, just as if it hadn't been standing still for hours or days, the golem moved to near the center of the open area, then saluted again.

Virgil took a position facing it, and saluted as well.

The coaching avatar said, "*En garde. Prêt. Allez!*" and the bout began.

It was amazing.

I hadn't fenced much with golems in college. Most of what we did was drills — thrust and parry, advance and retreat — and in a class it made more sense to have students practice the drills with one another. But there were a few golems of various vintages around, and students could practice with them when they weren't in use. They had levels that went up to 10, but at level 1, it could hold an advanced beginner to a draw, and at level 2, it could pretty much beat anyone who wasn't on the fencing team.

Once a few of my friends and I spent an hour seeing who could last longest at level 3, with the best of us — a classmate who qualified for the team the following year — lasting twelve seconds.

There was no reason to figure that the levels on that machine were the same as the levels on this one, but watching it fence with Virgil, it was easy to imagine that they might be. The golem moved with lightning speed, testing Virgil's defense comprehensively. At the same time, it parried with strength and efficiency. I didn't have nearly the experience to fully appreciate what was going on, but some bits did make an impression — the length and complexity of the phrases, the speed of Virgil's footwork and the way he always seemed to be perfectly balanced.

After perhaps five minutes of action that was almost all too fast for me to follow, Virgil said, "Now watch!" Then he launched a particularly complex sequence of moves ending (I later observed from the log) with an encircle, beat, beat feint, beat, and lunge.

And the lunge struck home, driving several centimeters into the golem's chest.

The golem acknowledged the touch, lowered his rapier, and became motionless.

"You see?" Virgil asked.

"See what?"

"It paused! After that last beat, the golem just froze for, I don't know, a quarter of a second. I could have touched it anywhere."

"Oh."

Virgil slashed the air with his rapier. "It's very frustrating. I can't beat the golem at level 88, but I can't get enough practice fighting at level 87 before this bug appears."

"I see," I said, watching the tip of his blade.

Seeing my expression, Virgil lowered his rapier, but smiled a slightly predatory smile. "Perhaps you could take a look and see what's wrong."

"Yes," I said, moving to the datapoint.

●   ●   ●

With some satisfaction, I was able to report to Virgil that I'd fixed the bug before dinner time.

"Really? What was wrong?"

"It was a memory management issue. The software always starts with the same level of skill at each level, so that practice sessions at any particular level are consistent. Starting at about level 40, the software learns during the course of the bout, so if you touch it with this or that maneuver, the same move probably won't work the next time.

"Starting at level 87, the golem begins to make use of data about the whole day's activity, drawn from the coaching software. This is supposed to simulate an opponent who's been paying attention — he knows about any bouts you fought earlier in the day, he knows if you lifted weights earlier in the day, if you had a big lunch, or if you went for a long run.

"There's a routine to take the whole day's activity and reduce it to a 'knowledge base' that the golem can use. If your legs are tired, he'll try to make you move more. If your arms are tired, he'll press harder there. If you had a tough ab workout, he'll work side-to-side, trying to make you twist. And so on.

"The bug is: that routine only gets called at the end of the day. In the meantime, the golem software uses the data in its raw form. It's run on very fast hardware, so that's usually okay. In the time it takes to decide exactly how to execute a parry, it is able to evaluate the whole raw database of the day's activity and decide on its next move. But, after a long day, there's just barely enough time — and sometimes, during a long, complex phrase, there's not quite enough time. It falls behind. Eventually, it reaches a point where it has finished the last move it has calculated, but has not yet determined what its next move should be, at which point it just stops and waits until it decides what to do next."

Virgil laughed. "A classic beginner's mistake."

"Yes," I said, remembering my teacher berating me for doing exactly that when one of my classmates interrupted a drill by doing something other than the assigned move. I was not to just stop. I was to do something appropriate.

"Anyway," I went on, "it's fixed."

"Fixed how?"

"Well, I call the raw database reduction routine before the match starts, so the software doesn't have to evaluate every single piece of raw data — which includes, for example, the force of each footstrike for your entire run, as well as your blood lactate levels for each second, and so on."

Virgil frowned, and I held up a hand. "I also fixed the 'classic beginner's mistake.' I took the evaluation of the accumulated day's data out of the main loop. I still *initiate* the evaluation each time, but if the routine hasn't finished when it's time to finalize the next move, the golem will leave it out of its calculations, and just go with its base skill level as of the beginning of the bout."

Now Virgil smiled. "It will learn over the course of a bout, but, if pressed too hard to keep up, it falls back on its training. Very realistic. Excellent! Is it ready to try?"

"It is," I said. "I installed the patch here, as well as sending it to Odessa Rae."

Virgil almost ran up the stairs to try it out.

I followed, just to watch the great man with his toy. He fenced with power, skill, and incredible endurance. When his breath was coming in gasps and his feet — somehow, after their perfect precision earlier — sometimes dragged a moment before hitting their mark, he fought all the harder.

The bout must have gone on for almost thirty minutes before Virgil, his face drawn with pain, failed to execute a perfectly straightforward parry. His legs obviously too tired to put him in exactly the right spot, his arm too tired to overcome the disadvantage of his slightly awkward position. The golem's thrust went home, bending sharply as the safety button struck Virgil low on the ribs.

Virgil stepped back and lowered his rapier.

I was almost tempted to help him off the floor, he was so obviously exhausted, but he didn't need my help. He made his way, only slightly unevenly, to the entrance to the room, then sat down at the top of the stairs.

"Can I bring you a glass of water?" I asked.

"That'd be nice. Thank you."

By the time I'd returned, he was much recovered.

"You're welcome to stay until morning," he said. "Cocktails. Dinner. Spend the night in the guest suite."

"No, thanks," I said. "I'm kind of in a hurry to get back."

"Oh? You have plans?"

"I do. I'm going to enter a match. Get my TSO rating."

•　　　•　　　•

I waited to be called to the fighting floor, knowing I was going to lose. I'd done something I hadn't done before: I'd reviewed the record of my opponent.

There were reasons I hadn't done that before. For one thing, everyone in the match was unrated, so there hadn't seemed much point.

But there's more than one way a player might be unrated. The fencer who had beaten me in the second round was unrated because he'd been too young for open match play.

My opponent in this bout was unrated because he'd retired from match play some twelve years earlier, and only bouts fought in the past ten years counted toward a rating.

His name was Delacroix. At the time of his retirement, the man had been rated 23rd in the world, down from 16th in the world the previous year. He was, of course, undefeated in this tournament.

The only other fencer in the match who might have put up a fight was the boy who'd beaten me in the second round. A match between them would probably have been pretty exciting — especially if the boy had permission from his minister to go flat-out without giving him the chance he'd given me.

Unfortunately for the tournament organizers, they'd fought in the third round, and Delacroix had won handily.

That was sad for the organizers. Delacroix was the only undefeated fencer, and so arguably already the winner. But, like the rest of us, he needed his five matches to get a new TSO rating.

The organizers needed to pair him with a fencer with only one loss. They couldn't pick the boy, because the rules prohibited repeating a previous match. There were three other people with only a single loss, but one was the woman I'd defeated in my previous match, and with her carotid injury, she was not yet cleared to fight. The only other one was the boy's previous opponent who had, unlike me, declined to yield. A few seconds later, he had taken a rapier to the heart and was even more out of the tournament than the woman.

So, as the only other player with only a single loss still standing, I found myself in the finals. In theory, there could be a three-way tie for first, if I won. In practice, once I lost, I'd be ranked in with the others who had won three bouts and lost two.

I was called to the floor. My opponent emerged a moment later. He was short, very lean, and moved like a dancer. His hair, cut close to his head, showed just a touch of gray at the temples. His torso displayed his musculature in stark relief. Less like a fitness model, more like an anatomical illustration.

He saluted me gravely, came *en garde*, and dispatched me in the first phrase — thrusting toward my chest, but allowing my frantic parry to divert the blade enough that it sank instead deep into the bicep of my sword arm. I retreated, but was unable to raise my blade, prompting the fightmaster to end the bout.

The medic put a dab of wound sealing gel on my arm and gave me an envelope with a few analgesic tablets, with instructions to take one every six hours as needed for pain.

Then it was time for the fingerprint.

They gave me credit for the time I struggled to get my rapier back up, so the official time of the bout was fourteen seconds, although it had actually been over in about three. It didn't make any difference to what I got paid, which was one denarius, same as for my previous loss.

•　　　•　　　•

The great man was just where he'd been before, sitting in the wide leather chair at the center of the throng.

I looked around the lodge's great room. It seemed different, and it took me a minute to realize that I simply hadn't noticed it before, my attention entirely on Virgil, holding court. Today I saw the big windows with their views of the mountains, the stone floors, the exposed wooden beams, the young people gathered around Virgil, hanging on every word.

A few people sat separate from the crowd. Two older men sat in the far corner, playing chess. A couple just a little younger engaged in a quiet conversation, their attention fully on one another. A woman about my age sat reading. She looked up for a moment when I looked her way, then returned her attention to her book.

I had come to tell Virgil that I had the rating he had dared me to get. But standing there, the urge to make my way through the throng, to sit at the feet of the great man, was totally absent.

I turned and went to the room where the breakfast buffet had been laid out before. Today, there was a snack buffet.

There was bread and cold cuts, which I used to make myself a sandwich. I took an apple from a bowl that might well have contained one of every kind of apple I'd ever heard of. I sat down at a small table by the window, a few steps from the buffet, my back to the throng.

While I was eating, the woman with the book came and served herself a snack, then approached my table. "May I join you?"

"Please," I said.

She set her book face down next to where she had put her plate. "I'm Jennifer Conroy," she said.

"Pleased to meet you," I said. "I'm Trevo Fisher."

"Oh, I know who you are," she said. "I expect everybody here knows. The question you asked is famous for going unanswered."

"Ah," I said. "I didn't know. Perhaps Odessa Rae thought it would be funny to suggest that I ask."

"Perhaps. Or perhaps there really is a good story there. But it falls into the category of 'Those who know aren't talking, and those who talk don't know.'"

We talked for a long time after that. Watched as the sun began to set. The east-facing wall of the canyon was in shadow, but the light of the setting sun shown on the west-facing wall of the canyon below us, and the reflected light illuminated the wall opposite, turning the wall we could see every shade of rose I could imagine.

I gestured toward the snack buffet. "Look at the apples," I said. Like the canyon walls, the red light of the setting sun showed off the colors of their peels gloriously.

"Oh!" Jennifer said. "They're lovely!"

Of course the party showed no sign of slowing, even after it was full dark outside.

I had planned to show Virgil my rating, hear his story, and then go to bed early. I had fought my final bout just the day before. My entire body was tired, and my arm was sore where I'd been wounded.

Somehow, talking to Jennifer energized me, and I found I could imagine staying up late talking with her. Then I found I could imagine instead taking her to bed with me. After a moment's thought, I proposed the idea, and found her not averse to it.

•　　•　　•

I awoke in the wee hours, my arm aching worse — probably due to excessively vigorous bedroom activities — and decided to take one of the analgesic tablets the medic had given me.

I went downstairs for a glass of water, and found Virgil alone in the kitchen, drawing his own glass of water from the tap.

"Trevo!" he said as I entered. "I saw you come in."

"Good morning," I said.

"I'm very pleased with the fix you made to my training golem. I put in a good word with Odessa Rae."

"Thank you."

"I saw your initial TSO rating," he said. "Pretty good, for a rookie fencer."

"Higher than I deserve," I admitted.

"Perhaps. Not higher than you can hold, if you hone your fencing skills."

"I've become dubious," I said. "About the audience. About the whole enterprise, really."

"I've never done it for the audience," Virgil said, taking a sip of water. "I do it to test myself."

I took my pill, finished my glass, and turned to go back up to where I had left Jennifer sleeping.

"Trevo, do you want to hear the story? What Max Mandrill said to me in that bout?"

I thought for a moment, not about whether I wanted to hear the story, but about how the whole room had looked so different when I'd entered — how I'd seen a room full of people, rather than just Virgil at the center.

"You knew," I told Virgil. "When you suggested I get my TSO rating. You knew that doing so would change me. That's why you wanted me to do it."

Virgil smiled. It was another version of the same predatory smile he'd given me when he'd been frustrated at the software bug that let him beat the gollum. "Maybe. Maybe I think the world needs more people who can set themselves a difficult task and then see it through."

He paused for just a moment, making sure I was looking him in the eye. "Or maybe I just thought getting a few pokes with a sharp sword was what you deserved for asking a nosy question."

I nodded. "Maybe so. Well. I did get poked with a sharp sword a couple of times, so sure. I guess I do want to hear the story."

Virgil smiled. "You've seen a video of the fight?" At my nod, he said, "Good. Then I can skip the build-up. Good ol' Max. When we came *corps a corps*, he put his mouth close to my ear, then said, 'Get a load of the bazoombas on the blonde behind me.'"

I pondered that for a moment, wondering why Odessa Rae thought it was a story worth hearing.

Then Virgil added, "I knew it was just a ploy to distract me, but damn if a minute later I didn't glance behind him. Of course, he was ready, came in low and got me in the groin. Took me out of the match."

"Was there even a blonde?" I asked.

"There was," Virgil said.

He looked at me then, and I could tell he was waiting for me to ask for more.

I decided not to.

I can learn from experience.

ABOUT THE AUTHOR

Philip Brewer stories often involve genetic engineering and money — perhaps not surprising, as everyone else in his family is some sort of naturalist and he has a degree in economics. Even before his former employer did him the great kindness of closing the site where he'd been working, giving him the opportunity to become a full-time writer, his stories often involved hard economic times.

Philip's work has appeared in *Asimov's Science Fiction*, *Futurismic*, *Redstone Science Fiction*, and *Lady Churchill's Rosebud Wristlet*. He speaks Esperanto and uses it for international communication.

YOU MIGHT ALSO ENJOY

BEST SERVED COLD

by Bob Schoonover

A dish of corporate greed served with a side of revenge.

CHOOSE YOUR TRUTH

by Jo Miles

Truth is obsolete. May the best lies win.

REDUCTION IN FORCE

by Steve Soult

A laid-off software engineer's only hope for salvation may be a revolutionary memory erasure procedure. But the price could be greater than he bargained for.

Available in digital and trade paperback editions from
Water Dragon Publishing
waterdragonpublishing.com